5/90

D1361472

Just Like Me

Also written by Patricia Lakin
and illustrated by Patience Brewster

Don't Touch My Room
Oh, Brother!

Just Like Me

by
Patricia Lakin

Illustrated by Patience Brewster

Little, Brown and Company

BOSTON   TORONTO   LONDON

For my grandmother who created the family whistle,
Gertrude Tennis Lakin,
And my friend Jane Lawrence Mali
With enormous thanks to
Lee Koenigsberg and Alison Cragin Herzig

— P. L.

To Katharyn, who turned out to be a great sister,
despite my early warnings (through the bathroom door)
to the contrary
And to " Jigglety Lady," for her original interpretation
of the "Crazy-Man" dance

— P. B.

Text copyright © 1989 by Patricia Lakin Koenigsberg
Illustrations copyright © 1989 by Patience Brewster

First Edition

Library of Congress Cataloging-in-Publication Data

Lakin, Pat.
  Just like me / by Patricia Lakin: illustrated by Patience
Brewster. — 1st ed.
     p. cm.
  Summary: Big brother Aaron, on the verge of leaving home for a class field trip, gives young Benji firm instructions to leave his things alone while he is gone, but then Aaron finds himself missing his little brother on the trip.
  ISBN 0-316-51233-8
  [1. Brothers — Fiction. 2. School excursions — Fiction.]
I. Brewster, Patience, ill. II. Title.
PZ7.L1586Ju 1989
[E] dc19   88-8375
                                                        CIP
                                                         AC

10 9 8 7 6 5 4 3 2 1

WOR

Published simultaneously in Canada
by Little, Brown & Company (Canada) Limited

Printed in the United States of America

I'm Leaving!

This is my room. But not for long.

My bags are packed. In the morning, I'm leaving!

I'm taking Max, my koala bear, with me.

I'm going on a winter class trip . . . to a farm.

For five whole days.

I'm glad.

I'll miss this house and my things and my lizard.

But I won't miss Benji.

Benji is a real pain in the neck.

He always wants to draw faces just like me.

But he can't, so he messes up my stuff and pretends
     he didn't.

Or he yells and does his "Crazy-Man" dance when I need
     things to be quiet.

He tells my jokes over and over again.

And he always interrupts when I'm talking.

When I go to bed, he begs for pillow fights.

"That's stupid," I tell him. "I always beat you."

And I do!

Before I know it, I'm the one that's in trouble.

But there's a problem.

Benji gets to be here for five whole days, all by himself.

So I'm leaving him a list.

I give the family whistle.

Benji knows it means, "Come quick!"

He does.

I read my list to him:

> Don't do anything fun while I'm away.
> No movies.
> No going out for pizza.
> No staying up late to watch something
>   special on television.

"Okay, Aaron," says Benji.
"I'm not done," I tell him.
I read the second page:

> Don't talk to my lizard.
> Don't touch my books or my
>   wood sculptures.
> Don't open my mail.
> Don't use my desk, my special paper, my
>   pencils, or my pencil sharpener.
> Don't eat any of my chocolate kisses.
>   I've counted them.
> Don't touch *any* of my things. I'll know!

Before I go, I look all around.

I memorize just how I left everything.

"Maybe I'll bring you a surprise," I tell my lizard. "So wait
for me."

"Okay, Aaron," says Benji. "I'll wait."

At the Farm

This is my room.

And Danny's and Nicky's and Ezra's room, too.

It's night and we unpack our bags with all our warm
  winter stuff.

I find a nice long twig in the corner of my drawer.

I tuck it in the back of my notebook. My lizard loves to
  climb twigs.

Danny starts a pillow fight.

Great!

All the pillows are flying now.

Nicky gets me with a tricky move from the side.

Then Ezra whomps me from the back.

I'm down! Those guys beat me! I can't believe it!

Then they say, "Nine o'clock. Lights out. Time for bed.
No talking."

I start to think about home.

What are they doing there now . . . without me?

It better not be anything fun, like staying up late, pizza
parties, or *anything* special.

Then I think . . . what if nobody misses me . . . not my
lizard, not *them* . . . not even Benji!

I grab Max very tight.

I scrunch down into my sleeping bag and turn toward
the wall.

I blink my eyes a lot.

I pretend I'm home now, talking to my lizard.

They say, "Six-thirty. Time to get up. Gather the eggs. And
    be gentle with the hens!"
Be gentle! Those hens attack us with their sharp little beaks!
I show Danny, Nicky, and Ezra how to do the "Crazy-Man"
    dance. It saves us.

Then they say, "Breakfast. And a nice time to share."

"Jokes?" I ask.

Danny tells three new knock-knock jokes.

We all laugh.

Then it's my turn. I tell my best joke.

The one Benji falls down crazy for.

"Knock-knock."

"Who's there?" they ask.

"Tennis," I say.

"Tennis who?" they ask.

"Oh, we know that one already," Ezra says. "Ten is a good
    age to be."

No one laughs.

"Nature time," they say. "Keep your eyes peeled for
    animals."

Who can look? I'm too busy trying to walk in
    these snowshoes.

But then I spot two rabbits sitting and eating berries.

I whistle. No one comes.

I forget.

My friends don't know what the whistle means.

"Dinner," they say. "Everyone has to make something."

"Can I make dessert?" I ask.

I pick out a recipe and get all the ingredients.

I measure, pour, stir, and moosh everything together.

The batter looks gross.

"Dessert ready?" they ask.

"Yes," I say.

"These cookies are the best," they say. "And loaded
    with chocolate."

After that, I have to make big batches at the farm
    every night.

I copy the recipe onto a clean page in my notebook.

I think about Benji. He's crazy about chocolate, just like me.

Before I know it, they say, "Time to pack up."
Danny, Nicky, Ezra, and I have one last pillow fight.
"This time," I tell my friends, "I'm watching for all
    your tricks."
Those guys still win!
I can't wait to have a pillow fight with Benji.
Before we get on the bus, the four of us do our "Crazy-Man"
    dance one more time.

"Who'd like to visit again?" they ask.
My hand shoots up.
I didn't know it would do that . . . without my
even thinking.

Coming Home

There are *Welcome Home, Aaron* signs all over the house.

Benji shows me the sign he made. It's a picture of our
　　whole family.

"And Aaron," he says, "I did the faces and hands just like
　　you taught me."

"They're good!" I tell him. "Benji, you're a good artist."

I take my bags into my room. Benji follows me.

The room looks bigger. I walk all around.

"Thirteen chocolate kisses," I count. "Good! Just what
　　I left."

"I missed you," I say to my lizard.

"I missed you, too," says Benji.

"Ya?" I ask.

"Yup," he answers.

"Everything seems okay," I tell him. "You sure you didn't
　　touch anything?"

"I'm sure," says Benji.

"What did you get to do while I was gone?" I ask him.

"Nothing," he says.

"Well," I tell him. "You did a good job staying away from
   my stuff."

Then I unpack my notebook and flip it to the last page.

"Here's your surprise," I tell my lizard.

"A twig?" asks Benji. "Yuck!"

"It's not for you," I tell him.

"Then where's my surprise?" he asks.

"Well, I didn't . . ."

"What'd you bring for me?" he interrupts.

"We were in the country, you know. There aren't any stores
    around . . . just cows, chickens, and . . ."

I toss my notebook onto my desk.

I remember my cookie recipe.

"But I did plan something," I tell him. "Special! Just
   for you."

"What?" he asks.

"You'll love it!" I tell him. "But you gotta stay out of
   the kitchen.

It'll take a while. So wait 'til I give the whistle."

"Okay, Aaron. I'll wait."

I take my notebook into the kitchen.

I get all the ingredients together.

Then I measure everything out.

I moosh the batter all up. This time I add extra
    chocolate bits.

I put the cookies in the oven and set the timer.

I flick on the oven light and look through the glass door.

The cookies are all spread out now. They look almost done.

I whistle.

Benji comes.

"Where's my surprise?" he asks.

"In here," I tell him. I point to the oven. "It's almost ready."

The two of us look at the cookies baking.

"You made them?" he asks. "By yourself?"

"Yup."

"How'd you know what to do?"

"I learned at the farm," I tell him. "I'll teach you how
    to make them, too, just like me!"

The bell rings.

I take the cookies out of the oven.

I put some on a plate.

Benji grabs one.

"Careful," I tell him. "They're still hot."

"They're great!" he says. "I love all the chocolate bits."

"Me, too," I tell him. "Come on, Benji. Let's have a pillow fight."

Aaron's Crazy-for-Chocolate-Chip Cookies

½ cup butter, softened
½ cup sugar
¼ cup brown sugar
1 egg
1 teaspoon vanilla
1 cup cake flour, sifted
½ teaspoon salt
½ teaspoon baking soda
1 package (6 oz.) semisweet chocolate bits
(add more if your brother's crazy about chocolate)

Directions:

Just mix everything together, drop by spoonfuls onto greased cookie sheet, and bake 10–12 minutes at 350°. Makes 2 dozen good-sized cookies.

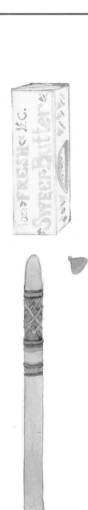

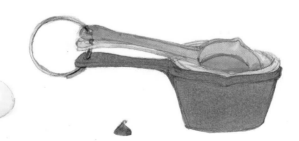